The Adventure of the Black Lady, and The Lucky Mistake

Aphra Behn

The Adventure of the Black Lady

A Novel

By Mrs. A. Behn.

1697

The Adventure of the Black Lady

About the beginning of the last June (as near as I can remember) Bellamora came to Town from Hampshire; and was oblig'd to lodge the first Night at the same Inn where the Stage-Coach set up. The next Day she took Coach for Covent-Garden, where she thought to find Madam Brightly, a Relation of her's; with whom she design'd to continue for about half a Year undiscover'd, if possible, by her Friends iin theCountry: And order'd therefore her Trunk, with her Cloaths, and most of her Money and Jewels, to be brought after her to Madam Brightly's, by a strange Porter whom she spoke to in the Street as she was taking Coach; being utterly unacquainted with the neat Practices of this fine City. When she came to Bridges-street, where inded her Cousin had lodged near three or four Years since; she was strangely surpriz'd that she cou'd not learn any thing of her; no, nor so much as meet with any one that had ever heard of her Cousin's Name. Till, at last, describing Madam Brightly to one of the house-keepers in that place, he told her, that there was such a kind of Lady, whom he had sometimes seen there about a Year and a half ago; but that he believ'd, she was married and remov'd towards So ho. In this Perplexity she quite forgot her Trunk and Money, etc. and wander'd in her Hackney-Coach all over St. Ann's Parish; inquiring for Madam Brightly, still describing her Person, but in vain; for no soul cou'd give her any Tale or Tidings of such a Lady. After she had thus fruitlesly rambled, till she, the Coachman, and the very Horses were e'en tir'd, by good Fortune for her, she happen'd on a private House, where lived a good, discreet, ancient Gentlewoman, who was fallen a little to decay, and was forc'd to let Lodgings for the best part of her Livelihood: From whom she understood, that there was such a kind of a Lady who had lain there somewhat more than a Twelve-month, being near three Months after she was married: But that she was now gone abroad with the Gentleman her Husband; either to the Play, or to take the fresh Air; and she believ'd, wou'd not return till Night. This Discourse of the good Gentlewoman's so elevated Belamora's drooping Spirits, that after she had begg'd the Liberty of staying there till they came home, she discharg'd the Coachman in all haste, still forgetting her trunk, and the more valuable Furniture of it.

When they were alone, Bellamora desired she might be permitted the Freedom to send for a Pint of Sack; which, with some little Difficulty, was at last allow'd her. They began then to chat for a matter of half an hour of things indifferent: And, at length the ancient Gentlewoman ask'd the Fair Innocent (I must not say Foolish) one, of what Country, and what her Name was: To both which she answer'd very directly and truly; tho' it might have prov'd, not discreetly. She then inquir'd of Bellamora if her Parents were living, and the Occasion of her coming to Town. The Fair Unthinking Creature replied, That her Father and Mother were both dead: And that she had escap'd from her Uncle, under pretence of making a Visit to a young Lady, her Cousin who was lately married, and liv'd above Twenty Miles from her Uncle's in the Road to London; and, that the Cause of her quitting the Country, was to avoid the hated Importunities of a Gentleman, whose pretended Love to her she fear'd had been her eternal Ruine. At which she wept and sigh'd most extravagantly. The discreet Gentlewoman endeavour'd to comfort her by all the softest and most powerful Argument in her Capacity; promising her all the friendly Assistance that she cou'd expect from her, during Bellamora's stay in Town; which she did with so much Earnestness and visible Integrity, that the pretty innocent Creature was going to make her a full and real Discovery of her imaginary, insupportable Misfortunes; and (doubtless) had done it; had she not been prevented by the Return of the Lady, whom she hop'd to have found her Cousin Brightly. The Gentleman her Husband just saw her within Doors, and order'd the Coach to drive to some of his Bottle- Companions; which gave the Women the better Opportunity of entertaining one another, which happen'd to be with some Surprize on all sides. As the lady was going up to her Apartment, the Gentlewoman of the House told her there was a young Lady in the Parlour, who came out o' the Country that very Day on purpose to visit her: The Lady stept immediately to see who it was, and Bellamora approaching to receive her hop'd for Cousin, stopp'd on the the suddain just as she came to her; and sigh'd out loud, Ah, Madam! I am lost. It is not your Ladyship I seek. No, Madam (return'd t'other) I am apt to think you did not intend me this Honour. But you are as welcome to me, as you could be to the dearest of your Acquaintance: Have you forgot me, Madam Bellamora? (continued she) that Name startled both the other: However, It was with a kind of Joy. Alas! Madam, (replied the young one I now remember that I have been so happy to have seen you: But where, and when, my Memory can't shew me. 'Tis indeed some Years since: (return'd the Lady) But of that another time. Mean while, if your are unprovided of a lodging, I dare undertake, you shall be welcom to this Gentlewoman. The Fair Unfortunate return'd her Thanks; and whilst a Chamber was preparing for her, the Lady entertain'd her in her own. About Ten a Clock they parted, Bellamora being conducted to her new Lodging by the Mistress of the House, who then left her to take what Rest she cou'd amidst her so many seeming Misfortunes; returning to the other Lady, who desir'd her to search into the Cause of Bellamora's Retreat to Town.

The next Morning the good Gentlewoman of the House coming up to her, found Bellamora almost drown'd in Tears, which by many kind and sweet Words she at last stopp'd; and asking whence so great Signs of Sorrow shou'd proceed, vow'd a most profound Secrecy if she wou'd discover to her their Occasion; which, after some little Reluctancy, she did, in this manner:

I was courted (said she) above three Years ago, when my Mother was yet living, by one Mr. Fondlove, a Gentleman of a good Estate, and true Worth; and one who, I dare believe, did then really love me: He continu'd his Passion for me, with all the earnest and honest Solicitations imaginable, till some Month's before my Mother's Death; who at that time, was most desirous to see me dispos'd of in Marriage to another Gentleman, of a much better Estate than Mr. Fondlove: But one, whose Person and Humour did by no means hit with my Inclinations: And this gave Fondlove the unhappy Advantage over me. For, finding me one Day all alone in my Chamber, and lying on my Bed, in as mournful and wretched a Condition, to my then foolish Apprehension, as now I am; He urg'd his Passion with such Violence and accursed Success for me, with reiterated Promises of Marriage, whenever I pleas'd to challeng 'em, which he bound with the most sacred Oaths and most dreadful Excrations; that partly with my Aversion to the other, and partly wih my Inclinations to pity him, I ruin'd my self. Here she relaps'd into a greater Extravagance of Grief than before; which was so extreme, that it did not continue long. When therefore, she was pretty well come to her self, the ancient Gentlewoman ask'd her, why she imagin'd her self ruin'd? To which she answer'd, I am great with Child by him (Madam) and wonder you did not perceive it last Night. Alas! I have not a Month to go: I am sham'd, ruin'd, and damn'd, I fear, for ever lost. O, fie, Madam, think not so: (replied Bellmora) I doubt not that he wou'd marry me; for, soon after my Mother's Death, when I came to be at my own Disposal, which happen'd about two Months after, he offer'd, nay, most earnestly sollicited me to it, which still he perseveres to do. This is strange! (return'd 'tother) And it appears to me to be your own Fault, that you are yet miserable. Why did you not, or why will you not consent

3

to your own Happiness? Alas! alas! (cry'd Bellamora) 'Tis the only thing I dread in this World: For, I am certain he can never love me after: Besides, ever since, I have abhorr'd the Sight of him: And this is the only Cause that obliges me to forsake my Uncle, and all my Friends and Relations in the Country, hoping this populous and publick Place to be most private, especially, (Madam) in your House, and in your Fidelity and Discretion. Of the last you may assure your self, Madam, (said t'other:) But what Provision have you made for the Reception of the young Stranger that you carry about you. Ah, Madam! (cry'd Bellamora) you have brought to mind another Misfortune: Then she acquainted her with the suppos'd Loss of her Money and Jewels, telling her withal, that she had but three Guinea's and some Silver left, and the Rings she wore, in her present Possession. The good Gentlewoman of the House told her, she wou'd send to inquire at the Inn where she lay the first Night she came to Town; for, (happily) they might give some account of the Porter to whom she had instrusted her Trunk; and withal repeated her Promise of all the help in her Power, and for that time left her much more compos'd than she found her. The good Gentlewoman went directly to the other Lady, her Lodger, to whom she recounted Bellamora's mournful Confession: At which the Lady appear'd mightily concern'd: And at last, she told her Land-lady, that she wou'd take Care that Bellamora should lie in according to her Quality: For, (added she) the Child (it seems) is my own Brothers.

As soon as she had din'd, she went to the Exchange and bought Child-bed Linen; but desir'd that Bellamora might not have the least Notice of it: And at her Return dispatch'd a Letter to her Brother Fondlove in Hantshire, with an Account of every particular; which soon brought him up to Town, without satisfying any of his or her Friends with the Reason of his sudden Departure; mean while, the good Gentlewoman of the House had sent to the Star-inn on Fish-street-hill, to demand the Trunk; which she rightly suppos'd to have been carried back thither: For, by good Luck, it was a Fellow that plyed thereabouts who brought it to Bellamora's Lodgings that very Night, but unknown to her. Fondlove no sooner got to London, but he posts to his Sister's Lodgings, where he was advis'd not to be seen of Bellamora till they had work'd farther upon her, which the Land-Lady began in this manner; she told her that her things were miscarried, and she fear'd lost; that she had but little Money her self, and if the Overseers of the poor (justly so call'd from their over-looking 'em) shou'd have the least Suspicion of a strange and unmarried Person, who was entertain'd in her House big with Child and so near her time as Bellamora was, she shou'd be troubled, if they cou'd not give Security to the Parish of twenty or thirty Pound that they shou'd not suffer by her, which she cou'd not; or otherwise, she must be sent to the House of Correction, and her Child to a Parish-Nurse. This Discourse one may imagine, was very dreadful to a Person of her Youth, Beauty, Education, Family and Estate: However, she resolutely protested, that she had rather undergo all this, than be expos'd to the Scorn of her Friends and Relations in the Country. The other told her then, that she must write down to her Uncle a farewell Letter, as if she were just going abroad the Pacquet-boat for Holland; that he might not send to inquire for her in Town, when he shou'd understand she was not at her new-married Cousin's in the Country, which accordingly she did, keeping her self a close Prisoner to her Chamber; where she was daily visited by Fondlove's Sister and the Land-Lady, but by no Soul else, the first dissembling the Knowledge she had of her Misfortunes. Thus she continued for above three Weeks; not a Servant being suffer'd to enter her Chamber, so much as to make her Bed, lest they shou'd take Notice of her great Belly: But for all this Caution, the Secret had taken Wind, by the means of an Attendant of the other Lady below, who had over-heard her speaking of it to her Husband. This soon got out 'o Doors and spread abroad, till it reach'd the long Ears of the Wolves of the Parish; who next day design'd to give her an ungrateful Visit: But Fondlove, by good Providence, prevented it; who, the Night before, was usher'd into Bellamora's Chamber by this Sister, his Brother-in-Law, and the Land-Lady. At the sight of him she had like to have swoon'd away: But he taking her in his Arms, began again, as he was wont to do, with Tears in his Eyes, to beg that she wou'd marry him e'er she was delivered; if not for his, nor her own, yet for the Child's sake, which she hourly expected; that it might not be born out of Wedlock, and so be made uncapable of inheriting either of their Estates; with a great many more pressing Arguments on all sides: To which at last she consented; and an honest officious Gentleman, whom they had before provided, was call'd up, who made an end of the Dispute: So to Bed they went together that Night; and next Day to the Exchange, for several pretty Businesses that Ladies in her Condition want. Whilst they were abroad, came the Vermin of the Parish, (I mean, the Overseers of the poor, who eat the Bread from 'em) to search for a young Black-hair'd Lady (for so was Bellamora) who was either brought to bed, or just ready to lie down. The Land-Lady shew'd 'em all the Rooms in her House, but no such Lady cou'd be found. At last she bethought her self, and led'em into her Parlour, where she open'd a little Closet-

The Lucky Mistake

By Mrs. A. Behn.

TO George Greenviel Esq;

SIR,

At this Critical Juncture, I find the Authors will have need of a
Protector, as well as the Nation, we having peculiar Laws and
Liberties to be defended as well as that, but of how different a
Nature, none but such Judges as you, are fit to determine; whatever
our Province be, I am sure it should be Wit, and you know what
Ellevated Ben says, That none can judge of Wit but Wit. Let the
Heroes toyl for Crowns and Kingdoms, and with what pretences
they please. Let the] Slaves of State drudge on for false and empty
Glories, troubling the repose of the World and ruining their own to
gain uneasy Grandure, whilst you, Oh! happyer Sir, great enough by
your Birth, yet more Illustrious by your Wit, are capable of enjoying
alone that true Felicity of Mind, which belongs to an absolutely
Vertuous and Gallant Man, by that, and the lively Notions of
Honour Imprinted in your Soul, you are above Ambition, and can
Form Kings and Heroes, when 'ere your delicate Fancy shall put you
upon the Poetical Creation.

You can make those Heroes Lovers too, and inspire 'em with] a
Language so Irresistable as may instruct the Fair, how easily you can
Conquer when it comes to your turn, to plead for a Heart, nor is
your delicate Wit the only Charm; your Person claims an equal share
of Graces with those of your Mind, and both together are capable of
rendering you Victorious, whereever you shall please to Address
'em, but your Vertue keeps you from those Ravages of Beauty, which
so wholly imploy the hours of the Rest of the Gay and Young, whilst
you have business more sollid, and more noble for yours.

I would not by this have the World imagine, you are therefore]
exempt from the tenderness of Love, it rather seems you were on
purpose form'd for that soft Entertainment, such an Agreement there

is between the Harmony of your Soul and your Person, and sure the Muses, who have so divinely inspir'd you with Poetic Fires, have furnisht you with that Necessary, Material (Love) to maintain it, and to make it burn with the more Ellevated Flame.

'Tis therefore Sir, I expect you will the more easily Pardon the the Dedicating to your idler hours (if any such you have) this little Amour, all that I shall say for it, is, that 'tis not Translation but] an Original, that has more of realty then fiction, if I have not made it fuller of intreague, 'twas because I had a mind to keep close to the Truth.

I must own, Sir, the Obligations I have to you, deserves a greater testimony of my respect, then this little peice, too trivial to bear the honour of your Name, but my increasing Indisposition makes me fear I shall not have many opportunities of this Kind, and shou'd be loath to leave this ungrateful World, without acknowledging my Gratitude more signally then barely by word of Mouth, and without wishing you all the happiness your merit and] admirable Vertues deserve, and of assuring you how unfeignedly I am (and how Proud of being) Sir,

> Your most obliged and
> most humble Servant,
> *A. Behn.*

The Luckey Mistake.

The River *Logre* has on its delightful Banks abundance of handsome Beautiful and Rich *Towns* and *Villages*, to which the Noble Stream adds no small Graces and Advantages, blessing their Fields with plenty, and their Eyes with a thousand Diversions. In one of these happily situated Towns, called *Orleance*, where abundance of People of the best Quality and Condition reside. There was a Rich Nobleman now retir'd from the busie Court, where in his Youth he had been bred, wearyed with the Toyls of Ceremony and Noise, to injoy that perfect Tranquillity of Life, which is no where to be found, but in retreat, a faithful Friend and a good Library; and as the admirable *Horace* says, in a little House and large Gardens, Count *Bellyaurd*, for so was this Noble Man call'd, was of this Opinion, and the rather because he had one only Son, *call'd Rinaldo* now grown to the Age of Fifteen, who having all the Excellent Qualities and Grace of Youth, by Nature; he would bring him up in all Vertues and Noble Sciences, which he believed the Gayety and Lustre of the Court might divert: he therefore in this retirement spar'd no Cost, to those that could instruct , 3, sig. B2] and accomplish him, and he had the best Tutors and Masters that could be purchased at Court: *Bellyaurd* making far less account of Riches than of fine Parts. He found his Son was capable of all Impressions, having a Wit suitable to his delicate Person, so that he was the sole Joy of his Life, and the Darling of his Eyes.

In the very next House, which joyned close to that of *Bellyuard's* there lived another Count, who had in his Youth been banisht the Court of *France* for some misunderstandings, in some high Affairs wherein he was concern'd, his Name was *De Pais*, a Man of great Birth, but no Fortune; or at least one not suitable to the Grandeur of his Original. And as it is most Natural for great Souls to be most proud, (if I may call a handsome Disdain by that Vulgar Name) when they are most deprest, so *De Pais* was more retir'd, more estrang'd from his Neighbours, and kept a greater distance, than if he had Enjoy'd all he had lost at Court, and took more Solemnity and State upon him, because he would not be subject to the reproaches of the World, by making himself familiar with it. So that he rarely visited, and was as rarely visited; and contrary to the Custom of those in *France*, who are easie of excess, and free of conversation, he kept his Family retir'd so close, that 'twas rare to see any of 'em, but when they went abroad, which was but seldom, they wanted nothing as to outward appearance, that was fit for his Quality, and was much above his Condition.

This old Count had two only Daughters, of exceeding Beauty, who gave the Generous Father ten thousand Torments, as often as he beheld them, when he consider'd their Extream Beauty, their , 5, sig. B3] fine Wit, their Innocence, Modesty, and above all, their Birth; and that he had not the Fortune to marry them according to their Quality; and below it he had rather see 'em laid in their silent Graves, then consent to; for he scorn'd the World should see him forced by his Poverty, to commit an Action below his Dignity.

There lived in a Neighbouring Town, a certain Nobleman, Friend to *De Pais*, call'd Count *Vernole*; A man of about forty Years of Age, of low Stature, Complexion very black and swarthy, lean, lame, extream proud and haughty; extracting of a Descent from the Blood Royal, not extreamly brave, but very glorious; he had no very great Estate, but was in Election of a greater, and of an Addition of Honour from the King, his Father having done most worthy Services against the *Hugonots*, and by the high Favour of *Cardinal Mazarine* was represented to his Majesty, as a Man related to the Crown, of great Name but small Estate; so that there was now nothing but great Expectations and Preparations in the Family of Count *Vernole* to go to Court, to which he dayly hop'd an Invitation or Command.

Vernole's Fortune being hitherto something akin to that of *De Pais*; there was a greater Correspondency between these two Gentlemen, then they had with any other Persons; They accounting themselves above the rest of the World, believ'd none so proper and fit for their Conversation, as that of each other; so that there was a very particular Intimacy between them, whenever they went abroad, they club'd their Train, to make one great Show, and were always together, , 7, sig. B4] bemoaning each others Fortune; that from so high a Descent, as one from Monarchs, by the Mothers side, and the other from *Dukes* of his side, they were reduc'd by Fate, to the degree of Private Gentlemen. They would often consult how to manage Affairs most to Advantage, and often *De Pais* wou'd ask Councel of *Vernole* , how best he should dispose of his Daughters, which now were about their Ninth Year the Eldest, and Eight the Youngest; *Vernole* had often seen these two Buds of Beauty, and already saw opening in *Atlante's* Face and Mind (for that was the Name of the Eldest, and *Charlot* the Youngest) a Glory of Wit and Beauty; which

cou'd not but one Day display it self with Dazling Lustre to the
wondering World

Vernole was a great *Vertuoso*, of a Humour, Nice, Delicate, Critical
and Opiniative; he had nothing of the *French mein* in him, but all the
Gravity of the *Don*; his ill Favour'd Person, and his low Estate, put
him out of Humour with the World, and because that should not
upbraid or reproach his Follies and Defects, He was sure to be before
hand with that, and to be always Satyric upon it, and lov'd to live
and act contrary to the Custom and Usage of all Mankind besides.

He was infinitely delighted to find a Man of his own Humour in *De
Pais*, or at least a Man that would be perswaded to like his so well, to
live up to it; and it was no little Joy and Satisfaction to him to find,
that he kept his Daughters in that Severity, which was wholly
agreeable to him, and so contrary to the Manner and Fashion of the
French of Quality; who allow all Freedoms, which to *Vernole's* rigid
Nature, seem'd , 9, sig. B5] as so many Steps to Vice, and in his
Opinion, the Ruiner of all Vertue and Honour in Woman kind. *De
Pais* was extreamly glad his conduct was so well interpreted which
was no other in him, than a proud Frugality; who, because they
could not appear, in so much Gallantry, as their Quality requir'd,
kept 'em retir'd, and unseen to all, but his particular Friends, of
which *Vernole* was chief.

Vernole never appear'd before *Atlante* (which was seldom,) but he
assum'd a Gravity and Respect, fit to have entertain'd a Maid of
twenty, or rather a Matron, of much greater Years and Judgment. His
Discourses were always of Matters of State or Phylosophy; and
sometimes when *De Pais* would laughing say, he might as well
entertain *Atlante*, with *Greek* and *Hebrew*, would reply gravely; you
are mistaken Sir, I find the Seeds of great and profound Matter in the
Soul of this Young Maid, which ought to be nourisht, now while she
was Young, and they will grow up to very great Perfection; I find
Atlante capable of all the Noble Vertues of the Mind, and am
infinitely mistaken in my Observations, and *Art* of *Phisiognomy*, if
Atlante be not born for greater things than her Fortune does now
promise, she will be very Considerable in the World, believe me, and
this will arrive to her perfectly from the Force of her Charms: *De Pais*
was extreamly overjoy'd to hear such good Prophesi'd to *Atlante*,
and from that time, set a sort of an Esteem upon her, which he did
not on *Charlot* his Younger; who by the perswasions of *Vernole*, he
resolv'd to put in a Monastery, that what he had might descend to

Atlante, not but he confess'd *Charlot* had Beauty, extreamly attractive, and a Wit that promis'd much, when it should be cultivated by Years and Experience; and would shew it self with great advantage, and Lustre in a Monastery; all this pleased *De Pais* very well, who was easily perswaded, since he had not a Fortune to marry her well in the World.

As yet *Vernole* had never spoke to *Atlante* of Love; nor did his Gravity think it Prudence, to discover his Heart to so Young a Maid, he waited her more sensible Years, when he could hope to have some return. And all he expected from this her tender Age, was by his daily converse with her, and the Presents, he made her suitable to her Years, to ingratiate himself insensibly into her Friendship and Esteem: Since she was not yet capable of Love, but even in that he mistook his Aim, for every day, he grew more and more disagreeable to *Atlante* , and would have been her Absolute Aversion, had she known, she had every day entertained a Lover, but as she grew in Years and Sense, he seemed the more despicable in her Eyes as to his Person, but as she had respect to his Parts and Qualities, she paid him all the Complaisance she could, and which was due to him; and it must be confess'd, tho' he had a stiff Formality in all he said and did, yet he had Wit and Learning, and was a great *Philosopher*; as much of his Learning, as *Atlante* was capable of attaining to, he made her Mistress of, and that was no small Portion, for all his Discourse was fine and easily comprehended, his Notions of *Philosophy* fit for *Ladies* ; and he took greater pains with *Atlante*, than any Master would have done with a Scholar; so that it was most certain, he added very great Accomplishments to her Natural Wit, and the more because she took a very great Delight in *Philosophy*; which very often made her Impatient of his coming: Especially when she had many Questions, to ask him concerning it, and she wou'd often receive him, with a Pleasure in her Face; which he did not fail to interpret to his own Advantage, being very apt to flatter himself, her Sister *Charlot* would often ask her, how she could give whole afternoons to so disagreeable a Man: What is it, said She, that charms you so, his Tawny Leather Face, his extraordinary high Nose, his wide Mouth and Eye-brows, that hang Lowring over his Eyes, his lean Carcass, and his Lame and Haulting Hips. But *Atlante* wou'd discreetly reply, if I must grant all you say of Count *Vernole* to be true yet he has a Wit and Learning, that will attone sufficiently for all those Faults you mention: A fine Soul is infinitely to be preferr'd to a fine Body; this decays, but that's Eternal; and Age that ruins one, refines the other;

Tho' possibly *Atlante* thought as ill of the Count, as her Sister; yet in Respect to him, she would not own it.

Atlante was now arriv'd to her thirteenth Year, when her Beauty, which every day increas'd, became the discourse of the whole Town; which had already gain'd her as many Lovers as had beheld her, for none saw her without Languishing for her, or at least but what were in very great Admiration of her, every body talkt of the young and charming *Atlante*, and all the Noble Men who had Sons (knowing the smallness of her Fortune and the lustre of her Beauty) would send them for fear of their being Charm'd with her, either to some other part of the World, or exhorted them, by way of precaution, to keep out of her sight: Old *Bellyuard* was one of these Wise Parents, and by a timely prevention as he thought of *Rinaldo's* falling in Love with *Atlante*, perhaps, was the occasion of his being so; he had before heard of *Atlante* and of her Beauty; but it had made no impressions on his Heart, but his Father no sooner forbid him Loving, than he felt a new desire Tormenting him, of seeing this lovely and dangerous young Person; he wonders at his unaccountable Pain, which daily solicits him within, to go where he may behold this Beauty; of whom he frames a thousand Ideas, all such as were most agreeable to him, but then upbraids his fancy for not forming her half so delicate as she was, and longs yet more to see her, to know how near she approaches to the Picture he has drawn of her in his Mind; and tho he knew she liv'd the next House to him, yet he knew also she was kept within like a Vow'd *Nun*, or with the severity of a *Spaniard* : And tho he had a Chamber which had a jetting Window that lookt just upon the the door of Monsieur *De Pays*, and that he would watch many hours at a time, in hope, to see them go out, yet he could never get a glimps of her; yet he heard she often frequented the Church of our *Lady*: thither then the young *Rinaldo* resolv'd to go, and did so two or three Mornings, in in which time to his unspeakable grief, he saw no Beauty appear that charm'd him, and yet he fancy'd that *Atlante* was there, and that he had seen her, that some one of those young Ladies, that he saw in the Church was she, tho he had no body to inquire of, and that she was not so fair as the World reported, for which he would often sigh as if he had lost some very great Expectation, however he ceas'd not to frequent this Church, and one day saw a young Beauty, who at first glimps made his Heart leap to his Mouth, and fell trembling again into its wonted place, for it immediately told him that that young Maid was *Atlante*, she was with her Sister *Charlot*, who was very handsom, but not comparable to *Atlante*. He fixt his Eyes upon her, as she kneel'd at the Altar,

13

which he never remov'd from that charming face as long as she remain'd there, he forgot all Devotion, but what he paid to her, he Ador'd her, he Burnt and Languish'd already for her, and found he must possess *Atlante*, or Dye; often as he gaz'd upon her he saw her fair Eyes lifted up towards his, where they often met, which she perceiving would cast hers down into her Bosom or on her Book, and blush as if she had done a Fault: *Charlot* perceiv'd all the Motions of *Rinaldo*, how he folded his Arms, how he sight, and how he gaz'd on her Sister; she took Notice of his Cloaths, his Garniture and every particular of his Dress, as young Girls use to do, and seeing him so very handsom, and so much better drest than all the young *Cavaliers* that were in the Church, she was very much pleas'd with him, and could not forbear saying in a low voice to *Atlante*, look, look, my Sister, what a pretty *Monsieur* yonder is, see how fine his Face is, how delicate his Hair, how gallant his Dress, and do but look how he gazes on you? This wou'd make *Atlante* blush anew, who durst not raise her Eyes for fear she should incounter his. While he had the pleasure to imagine they were talking of him, and he saw in the pretty Face of *Charlot*, that what he said was not to his disadvantage, and by the blushes of *Atlante*, that she was not displeas'd with what was spoken to her; he perceiv'd the young one importunate with her, and *Atlante* jogging her with her *Elbow*, as much as to say, hold your peace, all this he made a very kind Interpretation of, and was transported with Joy at the good *Omens*, he was willing to flatter his new Flame, and to Complement his young Desire, with a little Hope; but the divine Ceremony ceasing, *Atlante* left the Church, and it being very fair weather she walkt home, *Rinaldo*, who saw her going, felt all the Agonys of a Lover, who parts with all that can make him Happy, and seeing only *Atlante* attended with her Sister, and a Foot-man, following with their Books, he was a thousand times about to speak to 'em, but he no sooner advanc'd a step or two towards 'em, to that purpose (for he followed them) but his Heart fail'd, and a certain awe and reverence, or rather the fears and tremblings of a Lover, prevented him, but when he consider'd that possibly he might never have so favourable an opportunity again, he resolv'd anew, and call'd up so much Courage to his Heart as to speak to *Atlante*, but before he did so, *Charlot* looking behind her, saw *Rinaldo* very near to 'em, and cry'd out with a voice of Joy: Oh! Sister, Sister, look where the handsom *Monsieur*, is just behind us, sure he is some body of Quality, for see he has two Foot-men that follow him in just such Liveries, and so Rich, as those of our Neighbour *Monsieur Bellyaurd*: at this *Atlante* could not forbear, but before she was aware of it, turn'd her Head and lookt on *Rinaldo*, which incourag'd him to advance, and putting off his Hat, which he clapt under his Arm, with a low Bow, said, Ladies you are so slenderly attended, and so many Accidents arrive to the fair in the rude Streets, that I humbly implore you will permit me, whose Duty it is, as a Neighbour, to wait on you to your Door, Sir, said *Atlante* blushing, we fear no insolence, and need no Protector, or if we did we should not be so rude to take you out of your way to serve us; Madam, said he, my way lyes yours, I live at the next door and am Son to *Bellyaurd* your Neighbour; but Madam added he, if I were to go all my Life out of the way to do you Service, I should take it for the greatest Happiness, that could arrive to me, but Madam, sure a Man can never be out of his way, who has the Honour of so Charming Company, *Atlante* made no reply at this, but blusht and bow'd, but *Charlot* said, Nay Sir, if you are our Neighbour we will give you leave to Conduct us home; but pray Sir, how came you to know we are your Neighbours, for we never saw you before to our knowledge. My pretty *Mis*, reply'd *Rinaldo*, I knew it from the transcendent Beauty that appear'd in your Faces and fine Shapes, for I have heard there was no Beauty in the World like that of *Atlante's*, and I no sooner saw her but my Heart told me it was she; Heart, said *Charlot*, Laughing, why does Heart use to speak; the most intelligibly of any thing, reply'd *Rinaldo*, when 'tis tenderly toucht, when 'tis charm'd and transported, at these words he sight, and *Atlante* to his extream satisfaction blusht; toucht, charm'd and transported, said *Charlot*, what's that? and how do you do to have it be all these things? for I would give any thing in the World to have my Heart speak: Oh! said *Rinaldo*, your Heart is too young, it is not yet arriv'd to the Years of speaking, about thirteen or fourteen it may possibly be saying a thousand soft things to you, but it must first be inspir'd by some Noble Object, whose Idea it must retain; what reply'd, this pretty Pratler, I'le warrant I must be in Love? Yes, said *Rinaldo*, most passionately, or you will have but little Conversation with your Heart, Oh! reply'd she, I am afraid the pleasure of such a Conversation will not make me amends for the Pain that Love will give me, that, said *Rinaldo*, is according as the Object is kind, and as you hope, if he Love, and you hope you will have a double Pleasure, and in this how great an advantage have you fair Ladies above us Men: 'tis almost impossible for you to Love in vain, you have your choice of a thousand Hearts which you have subdu'd, and may not only chuse your Slaves but be assur'd of 'em; without speaking you are belov'd, it needs not cost you a sigh or tear; but unhappy Man is often destin'd to give his Heart, where it is not regarded, to sigh, to weep and languish without any hope of Pitty. You speak so feelingly, Sir said *Charlot*, that I am afraid this is your Case; Yes, Madam, reply'd *Rinaldo*, sighing, I am that unhappy Man; indeed 'tis pitty said she, pray how long have you been so? ever since I heard of the charming *Atlante* , reply'd he, sighing again, I ador'd her Character, but now I have seen her, I dye for her; for me, Sir, said *Atlante* (who had not yet spoke, this is the common compliment of all the young Men, who pretend to be Lovers, and if one should pitty all those sighers, we shou'd have but very littel left for our selves; I believe, said *Rinaldo*, there are none that tell you so, who do not mean as they say, yet among all those adorers and those that say they will dye for you, you will find none will be so good as their words as *Rinaldo* , perhaps said *Atlante*, of all those who tell me of dying, there are none that tell it with so little reason as *Rinaldo*, if that be your Name Sir; *Madam* it is, said he, and who am Transported with an unspeakable joy, to hear those last words from your fair mouth, and let me Oh! Lovely *Atlante*, assure you that what I have said, are not words of Course, but proceed from a heart that has vow'd it self, eternally yours, even before, I had the happiness to behold this Divine Person, but now that my Eyes have made good all my heart before imagin'd, and did but hope, I swear I will dye a Thousand deaths, rather then violate what I have said to you, that I adore you, that my Soul and all my faculties are charm'd with your Beauty and Innocence, and that my Life and Fortune, not inconsiderable, shall be laid at your Feet: this he spoke with a fervency of passion, that left her no doubt of what he had said; yet she blusht for shame, and a little angry at her self, for suffering him to say so much to her, the very first time she saw him, and accused herself for giving him any incouragement: and in this confusion she reply'd, Sir, you have said too much to be believ'd, and I cannot imagin so short an acquaintance can make so considerable an Impression, of which confession I , 27, sig. C2] accuse my self much more than you, in that I did not only harken to what you said, without forbiding you to entertain me at that rate, but for unheedily speaking something, that has incourag'd this boldness; for so must I call it in a Man, so great a stranger to me: *Madam*, said he, if I have offended by the suddainess of my presumptious discovery, I beseech you to consider my reasons for it, the few opportunities I am like to have, and the impossibility of waiting on you, both from the severity of your Father and mine; who 'ere I saw you, warn'd me of my Fate, as if he foresaw, I should fall in Love as soon as I should chance to see you; and for that reason has kept me closer to my Studies, than hitherto I have been, and from that time I began to feel a Flame, which was kindled by report alone, and the Description my Father gave of your wonderous and dangerous Beauty: therefore *Madam* , I have not suddainly told you of my passion, I have been long your Lover, and have long Languisht without telling of my Pain, and you ought to Pardon it now, since it is done with all the respect and Religious Awe, that 'tis possible for a heart to deliver and unload it self in; therefore *Madam*, if you have by chance uttered any thing, that I have taken advantage or hope from, I assure you 'tis so small, that you have no reason to repent it; but rather if you wou'd have me live, send me not from you, without a confirmation of that little hope; see *Madam*, said he, more earnestly and trembling, see we are almost arriv'd at our homes, send me not to mine in a despair, that I cannot support with Life, but tell me I shall be , 29, sig. C3] blest with your Sight sometimes in your Balcony, which is very near to a jetting Window in our House, from whence I have sent many a longing look towards yours, in hope to have seen my Souls Tormenter; I shall be very unwilling, said she, to enter into an intreague of Love, or Friendship with a Man, whose Parents will be averse to my happiness, and possibly mine as refractory, though he cannot but know such an Alliance wou'd be very considerable; my Fortune being not suitable to yours, I tell you this, that you may withdraw in time from a Engagement, in which I find there will be a great many Obstacles Oh! *Madam* reply'd *Rinaldo*, sighing, if my Person be not disagreeable to you; you will have no cause to fear the rest, 'tis that I dread, and that which is all my fear, he sighing beheld her with a Languishing look, that told her, he expected her answer, when she reply'd, Sir, if that will be Satisfaction enough for you at this time, I do assure you, I have no aversion for your Person, in which I find more to be vallu'd than in any I have yet seen, and if what you say be real, and proceed from a heart truly affected, I find in spight of me, you will oblige me to give you hope.

They were come so near their own Houses, that he had not time to return her any answer, but with a low bow he acknowledg'd her Bounty, and exprest the joy her last words had given him, by a look that made her understand, he was charm'd and pleas'd, and she bowing to him, with an Air of satisfaction in her Face, he was well assured, there was nothing to be seen so lovely as she then appear'd, and left her to go into her own House, but till she was out of , 31, sig. C4] sight, he had not Power to stir, and then sighing retired to his own Apartment, to think over all that had past between them, he found nothing but what gave him a thousand joys, in all she had said; and he blest this happy day, and wonder'd how his Stars came so kind, to make him in one hour at once see *Atlante*, and have the

17

happiness to know from her own mouth, that he was not disagreeable to her, yet with this satisfaction, he had a thousand thoughts mixt, which were tormenting, and those were the fear of their Parents, he foresaw from what his Father had said to him already, that it would be difficult to draw him to a consent of his Marriage with *Atlante*, these joys and fears were his companions all the Night, in which he took but little rest. Nor was *Atlante* without her inquietudes: she found *Rinaldo* more in her thoughts, than she wisht, and a suddain change of humour, that made her know something was the matter with her, more then usual; she calls to mind *Rinaldo's* speaking of the conversation with his heart, and found hers wou'd be tatling to her, if she would give way to it, and yet the more she strove to avoid it, the more it importun'd her, and in spight of all her resistance, would tell her, that *Rinaldo* had a thousand charms, it tells her that he Loves and adores her, and that she would be the most cruel of her Sex, should she not be sensible of his passion, she finds a thousand graces in his Person and Conversation, and as many advantages in his Fortune, which was one of the most considerable in all those Parts, for his Estate exceeded that of the most Noble Men in *Orleance*, and she imagins she should be the most , 33, sig. C5] Fortunate of all Woman-kind in such a Match; with these thoughts, she imploy'd all the hours of the Night, so that she lay so long in Bed the next day, that Count *Vernole*, who had invited himself to Dinner, came before she had quitted her Chamber, and she was forc'd to say she had not been well; he had brought her a very fine Book, newly come out, of *Delicate Philosophy*, fit for the study of Ladies, but he appeared so disagreeable to that heart, wholly taken up with a new and fine Object, that she could now hardly pay him that civility, she was wont to do, while on the otherside, that little State and Pride *Atlante* assum'd, made her appear the more charming to him, so that if *Atlante* had no mind to begin a new Lesson of *Philosophy*, while she fancy'd her thoughts were much better employ'd, the *Count* every moment expressing his tenderness and passion, had as little an inclination to instruct her, as she was to be instructed; Love had taught her a new Lesson, and he would fain teach her a new Lesson of Love, but fears it will be a diminishing of his *Gravity* and *Grandure*, to open the Secrets of his heart to so young a Maid, he therefore thinks it more agreeable to his Quality and Years, being about forty, to use her Father's Authority in this Affair, and that it was sufficient for him, to declare himself to *Monsieur De Pais*, who he knew would be Proud of the Honour he did him sometime past, before he could perswade himself, even to declare himself to her Father; he fancies the little coldness and Pride he saw in *Atlante's* Face, which was not usual, proceeded from some discovery of Passion, which his Eyes had made, or now and then a Sigh, that unawares broke forth, and accuses himself of a Levity below his Quality and the Dignity of his Wit and Gravity: and therefore assumes a more rigid and formal Behavior then he was wont, which render'd him yet more disagreeable than, before; and 'twas with greater pain than ever, she gave him that respect which was due to his Quality.

Rinaldo after a restless Night, was up very early in the Morning, and tho' he was not certain of seeing his Adorable *Atlante* , he drest himself with all that care, as if he had been to have waited on her, and got himself into the Window, that overlooks *Monsieur De Pays* his Balcony, where he had not remain'd long, before he saw the pretty *Charlot* come into it, not with any design of seeing *Rinaldo*, but to look and gaze about her a little, *Rinaldo* saw her, and made her a very low Reverence, and found some disordered Joy on the sight of even *Charlot*, since she was Sister to *Atlante*, he call'd to her (for the Window was so near her, he could easily be heard by her) and told her he was infinitely indebted to her Bounty, for giving him an opportunity yesterday of falling on that discourse, which had made him the happiest Man in the World, he said, if she had not by her agreeable Conversation incourag'd him, and drawn him from one word to another, he should never have had the confidence to have told *Atlante*, how much he ador'd her; I am very glad, reply'd *Charlot*, that I was the occasion of the beginning of an Amour which was displeasing to neither one nor to the other, for I assure you for your comfort, my Sister nothing but thinks on you, we lye together and you have taught her already to sigh so, that I could not sleep for her; at this his Face was covered over with a rising Joy which his Heart could not contain, and after some more discourse in which this innocent Girl discover'd more then *Atlante* wisht she should, he besought her to become his Advocate, and since she had no Brother, to give him leave to assume that Honour, and call her Sister, thus by degrees he flattered her into a consent of carrying a Letter from him to *Atlante*, which she who believ'd all as innocent as her self, and being not forbid to do so, immediately consented to, when he took his Pen and Ink that stood in the Window with Paper, wrote *Atlante* this following Letter.

Rinaldo to Atlante.

If my Suit be so severe as to deny me the happiness of sighing out my pain and passion daily at your Feet, if there be any Faith in the Hope you were pleas'd to give me (as 'twere a Sin to doubt,) do not, Oh Charming Atlante! suffer me to Languish both without beholding you, and without the blessing of now and then a Billet in answer to those that shalt daily assure you of my eternal Faith and Vows, 'tis all I ask till Fortune and our Affairs shall allow me the unspeakable satisfaction of Claiming you, yet if your Charity can sometimes afford me a sight of you, either from your Balcony in the Evening, or at Church in the Morning, it would save me from that Dispair and Torment, which must possess a Heart so unassured as that of,

> *Your Eternal Adorer*
> *Rin. Bellyuard.*

He having Writ and Seal'd this, tost it into the Balcony to *Charlot*, having first look'd about to see if none perceiv'd them; she put it in her Bosom and ran into her Sister, whom by chance she found alone, *Vernole* having taken *De Pays* into the Garden to Discourse with him concerning the sending *Charlot* to the Monastery, which work he desir'd to see perform'd, before he declar'd his intentions to *Atlante*, for among all his other good qualities, he was very avaritious, and as fair as *Atlante* was he thought she would be much fairer with the Addition of *Charlot's* Portion: this Affair of his with *Monsieur De Pays* gave *Charlot* an opportunity of delivering her Letter to her Sister, who no sooner drew it from her Bosom, but *Atlante's* Face was covered over with Blushes, for she imagin'd from whence it came, and had a secret Joy in that imagination; tho' she thought she must put on the Severity and Niceness of a Virgin, who would not be thought to have surrender'd her Heart with so small an Assault, and the first too; so she demanded from whence *Charlot* had that Letter, who reply'd with joy, from the fine Young Gentleman, our Neighbour; at which *Atlante* assum'd all the gravity she could, to chide her Sister, who reply'd, well Sister had you this day seen him, you would not have been angry to have receiv'd a Letter from him, he lookt so handsom, and was so richly drest, ten times finer then he was Yesterday; and I promis'd him you should read it, therefore pray let me keep my word with him, and not only so, but carry him an Answer, well, said *Atlante*, to save your Credit with *Monsieur Rinaldo*, I will read it, which she did and finisht with a sigh; while she was reading it, *Charlot* ran into the Garden to see if they were not likely to be surpris'd, and finding the *Count*, and her Father, set in an

Arbour in deep Discourse, she brought Pen, Ink and Paper to her Sister, and told her she might Write without the fear of being disturb'd, and urg'd her so long to what was enough her inclination, she at last obtain'd this Answer;

Atlante to Rinaldo.

Charlot, your little importunate Advocate has at last subdu'd me to a Consent of returning you this; she has put me on an Affair, which I am wholly unacquainted with; and you ought to take this very kindly from me since 'tis the very first time I ever Writ to one of your Sex, tho' perhaps I might with less danger have done it to any other Man; I tremble while I Write, since I dread a Correspondence of this Nature, which may insensibly draw us into an inconvenience, and engage me beyond the limits of that Nicety, I ought to preserve; for this way we venture to say a thousand little kind things which in Conversation we dare not do, for now none can see us blush; I am sensible I shall this way put my self too soon into your power, and tho' you have abundance of Merit, I ought to be asham'd of Confessing, I am but too sensible of them;—but hold—I shall discover for your Repose (which I would preserve) too much of the Heart of

Atlante.

She gave this Letter to *Charlot*, who immediately ran into the Balcony with it, where she still found *Rinaldo* in a Melancholly posture, leaning his Head on his Hand, she show'd him the Letter, but was afraid to toss it to him, for fear it might fall to the ground, so he ran and fetcht a long Cane which he cleft at one End, and holding it where she put the Letter into the Cleft, and staid not to hear what he said to it, but never was Man so transported with Joy, as he was at the reading of this Letter; it gives him new wounds; for to the generous, nothing obliges Love so much as Love; tho 'tis now too much the Nature of that inconstant Sex to cease to Love as soon as they are sure of the Conquest. But it was far different with our *Cavalier* , he was the more inflam'd by imagining he had made some impressions on the Heart of *Atlante*, and kindled some sparks there, that in time might increase to something more; so that he now resolves to dye hers, and considering all the Obstacles that may possibly hinder his Happiness, he found none but his Fathers obstinacy, perhaps occasion'd by the meanness of *Atlante's* Fortune, to this he urg'd again that he was his only Son, and a Son whom he lov'd equal to his own Life; and that certainly as soon as he should behold him dying for *Atlante*, which if forc'd to quit he must be, that then he believ'd the tenderness of so fond a Parent, would break forth into Pitty and Compassion, and plead within for his Consent: these were the thoughts that flattered this Young Lover all the day, and whether he were Riding the great Horse, or at his Study of Philosophy, or Mathamaticks, Singing or Dancing, whatever other Exercise his Tutors ordered, his thoughts were continually on *Atlante*, and now he profited no more; whatever he seem'd to do, every day he fail'd not to Write to her by the Hand of the kind *Charlot*, who young, as she was, had conceiv'd a very great Friendship for *Rinaldo*, and fail'd not to fetch his Letters, and bring him Answers such as he wisht to receive; but all this did not satisfy our impatient Lover, absence kill'd, and he was no longer able to support himself without a sight of this Adorable Maid; he therefore implores she will give him that satisfaction, and she at last grants it, with a better Will than he imagin'd, the next day was the appointed time, when she would under pretence of going to Church give him an assignation, and because all public places were dangerous, and might make a great noice, and they had no private place to trust to, *Rinaldo* under pretence of going up the River in his Pleasure Boat, which he often did, sent to have it made ready against the next day, at ten of the Clock; this was accordingly done and he gave *Atlante* Notice of his design of going an hour or two on the River, in his Boat, which lay near such a place, not far from the Church: she and *Charlot* came thether, and because they durst not come out, without a Footman or two, they taking one, sent him with a *how do ye*, to some Young Ladies, and told him he should find them at Church; so getting rid of their spy, they hastned to the River side, and found a Boat and *Rinaldo* waiting to carry them on Board his little Vessel, which was richly adorn'd, and a very handsom Collation ready for them of Cold Meats, Sallads and Sweetmeats; as soon as they were come into the Pleasure Boat, unseen of any, he kneel'd at the Feet of *Atlante*, and there utter'd so many passionate and tender things to her, with a voice so trembling and soft, with Eyes so Languishing, and a Fervency and Fire so sincere, that her young Heart wholly uncapable of Artifice, could no longer resist such Language, and such Looks of Love, she grows tender, and he perceives it in her fine Eyes, who could not dissemble, he reads her Heart in her Looks, and found it yielding apace, and therefore Assaults it anew with fresh forces of Sighs and Tears, he implores she would assure him of her Heart, which she could no other way do then by yielding to Marry him; he would carry her to the next Village, there consummate that Happiness, without which he was able to live no longer, for he had a thousand Fears, that some other Lover was, or would, suddainly be provided for her, and therefore he would make sure of her, while he had this opportunity; and to that end he answered all the Objections, she could make, to the contrary: but ever when he nam'd Marriage, she trembled with fear of doing something that she fancy'd she ought not to do without the Consent of her Father, she was sensible of the Advantage, but had been so us'd to a strict Obedience, that she could not without Horror think of Violating it, and therefore besought him, as he valu'd her Repose, not to urge her to that, and told him further that if he fear'd any Rival, she would give him what other Assurance and Satisfaction he pleas'd, but that of Marriage, which she could not consent to, till she knew such an Aliance would not be Fatal to him; for she fear'd as passionately as he lov'd her, when he should find she had occasion'd him the loss of his Fortune, or his Fathers Affection, he would grow to hate her; tho' he answered to this, all that a fond Lover could urge, yet she was resolv'd, and he was forc'd to content himself with obliging her by his Prayers and Protestations, his Sighs and his showers of Tears to a Contract, which they solemnly made each other, vowing on either side, that they would never Marry any other, this being solemnly concluded, he assum'd a Look more Gay and Contented than before, he presented her a very rich Ring, which she durst not put on her Finger, but hid it in her Bosom: and beholding each other now as Man and Wife, she suffer'd him all the decent Freedoms he could wish to take, so that the hours of this Voyage seem'd the most soft and charming of his Life, and doubtless they were so, every touch of *Atlante* transported him, every look pierc'd his Soul, and he was all Raptures of Joy, when he consider'd this charming lovely Maid was his own.

Charlot all this while was gazing above Deck, admiring the motion of the little Vessel, and how easily the Wind and Tide bore her up the River; she had never , 51, sig. D2] been in any thing of this Kind before, and was very well pleased and entertain'd, when *Rinaldo* call'd her down to eat, where they enjoy'd themselves as well as was possible, and *Charlot* was wondering to see such a Content in their Eyes.

But now they thought it was high time for them to return, they fancy the Footman missing them at Church, would go home and Alarm their Father, and the Knight of the ill Favour'd Countenance, as *Charlot* call'd Count *Vernole*, whose severity put their Father on a greater restriction of them than naturally he would do of himself: At the Name of this Count, *Rinaldo* chang'd colour, fearing he might be some Rival, and asked *Atlante*, if this *Vernole* was akin to her, she answered No; but was a very great Friend to her Father, and one who from their Infancy, had had a particular concern for their breeding, and was her Master for *Philosophy*. Ah! reply'd *Rinaldo* sighing, this Man's concern must proceed from something more than Friendship for her Father, and therefore conjured her to tell him, whether he were not a Lover? A Lover reply'd *Atlante* ; I assure you, he is a perfect *Antidote* against that Passion; and tho' she suffered his Ugly Presence now, she should loath and hate him, should he name but Love to her.

She said, she believ'd she need not fear any such Persecution, since he was a Man, who was not at all Amorous, that he had too much of the *Satyr* in his Humour to harbour any softness there: and Nature had form'd his Body to his Mind, wholly unfit for Love; and that he might set his Heart absolutely at rest, she assur'd him her Father had never yet propos'd any marriage to her, tho' many , 53, sig. D3] advantagious ones are offer'd him every day.

The Sails being turn'd to carry them back from whence they came; after having discours'd of a thousand things, and all of Love and Contrivance to carry on their Mutual Design, they with Sighs parted, *Rinaldo* staying behind in the Pleasure Boat, and they going a Shore in the Whery, that attended; after which he cast many an Amorous and sad Look, and perhaps was answer'd by those of *Atlante*.

It was past Church time two or three Hours; when they arriv'd at Home wholly unprepared with an excuse, so Absolutely was *Atlante's* Soul possest with Softer Business. The first Person they met withal was the Footman, who open'd the Door, and began to cry out, how long he had waited in the Church, and how in Vain; without giving them time to reply, *De Pais* came towards 'em, and with a Frowning Look, demanded where they had been? *Atlante* who was not accustomed to Excuses and Untruth, was a while at a stand, when *Charlot* with a Voice of Joy cryed out, Oh Sir we have been a Board of a fine little Ship: At this *Atlante* blusht fearing she would tell the Truth. But she proceeded on, and said; that they had not been above a Quarter of an Hour at Church, when the *Lady* — with some other *Ladies* and *Cavaliers*, were going out of the Church, and that spying them, they wou'd needs have them go with 'em; my Sister Sir, continued she, was very loath to go, for fear you should be angry, but my *Lady* — was so importunate with her on one side, and I on the other; because I never saw a little Ship in my Life, that at last

we prevailed with her, therefore good Sir, be not angry. He promised
, 55, sig. D4] them he was not, and when they came in, they found
Count *Vernole* , who had been inspiring *De Pais* with Severity, and
councel'd him to chide the Young *Ladies*, for being too long Absent,
under Pretence of going to their Devotion, nor was it enough for him
to set the Father on, but himself with a Gravity, where Concern and
Malice were both apparent, reproacht *Atlante* with Levity, and told
her, he believ'd she had some other Motive, then the Invitation of a
Lady, to go on Ship-board, and that she had too many Lovers, not to
make them doubt that this was a Design'd thing, and that she had
heard Love from some one, for whom it was designed: To this she
made him but a short reply, that if it was so, she had no reason to
conceal it, since she had Sense enough to look after herself, and if
any Body had made Love to her, he might be assur'd it was some
one, whose Quality and Merit deserv'd to be heard; and with a Look
of Scorn, she past on to another Room, and left him silently raging
within with Jealousie. Which if before she tormented him, this
Declaration increas'd it to a Pitch not to be conceal'd. And this Day
he said so much to the Father, that he resolv'd forthwith to send
Charlot to a *Nunery*, and accordingly the next Day, he bid her prepare
to go: *Charlot*, who was not yet arrived to the Years of Distinction,
did not much regret it, and having no trouble, but leaving her Sister,
she prepared to go to a *Nunery* not many Streets from that where she
dwelt. The *Lady Abbess* was her Father's Kins-woman, and had
treated her very well, as often as she came to visit her, so that with
satisfaction enough, she was condemned to a *Monastick* , 57, sig. D5]
Life, and was now going for her Probation Year: *Atlante* was
troubled at her departure, because she had now no body to bring
and to carry Letters between *Rinaldo* and she: However she took her
leave of her, and promis'd to come and see her, as often as she
should be permitted to go abroad, for she fear'd now some
constraint extraordinary would be put upon her, and so it happen'd.

Atlante's Chamber was that to which the Balcony belong'd, and
though she durst not appear there in the day time, she could in the
Night, and that way give her Lover as many hours of her
conversation, as she pleased without being perceived: but how to
give *Rinaldo* notice of this she could not tell, who not knowing
Charlot was gone to a *Monestary*, waited many days at his Window to
see her; at last they neither of them knowing who to trust with any
Message, one day when he was, as usual, upon his watch, he saw
Atlante step into the Balcony, who having a Letter, in which she had
put a peice of Led, she tost it into his Window, whose Casement was

open, and run in again unperceived by any but himself, the Paper contain'd only this.

My Chamber is that which looks into the Balcony, from whence, tho' I cannot converse with you in the day, I can at Night when I am retired to go to Bed, therefore be at your Window, Farewel.

There needed no more to make him a dilligent watcher, and accordingly she was no sooner retired to her Chamber, but she would come into the Balcony, where she fail'd not to see him attending at his Window, this happy contrivance was thus carry'd on for many Nights, where they entertain'd one another, with all the indearment that two hearts could dictate, who were perfectly united and assured of each other, and this pleasing Conversation would often last till day appeared, and forced 'em to part.

But old *Belyuard* perceiving his Son frequent that Chamber more then usual, fancy'd something extraordinary must be the the cause of it, and one Night asking for his Son, his *Vallet* told him he was gone into the great Chamber, so this was called: *Belyuard* asked the *Vallet* what he did there, he told him he could not tell, for often he had lighted him thither, and that his Master would take the Candle from him at the Chamber Door, and suffer him to go no further; tho' the Old Gentleman could not imagin, what Affairs he could have alone every Night in that Chamber, he had a curiosity to see, and one unlucky Night, putting off his shoes he came to the Door of the Chamber which was open, he entered softly, and saw the Candle set in the Chimney, and his Son at a great open Bay Window; he stopt a while to wait when he would turn, but finding him immovable, he advanced something further, and at last heard the soft Dialogue of Love, between him and *Atlante*, whom he knew to be she, by his often calling her by her Name in their discourse, he heard enough to confirm him how Matters went, and unseen as he came, he returned, full of indignation and thought how to prevent so great an Evil, as this Passion of his Son might produce, at first he thought to round him severely in the Ear about it, and upbraid him for doing the only thing he had thought fit to forbid him, but then he thought that would but terrify him for a while, and he would return again, where he had so great an inclination if he were near her; he therefore resolves to send him to *Paris*, that by absence he might forget this young Beauty, that had charmed his Youth: therefore without letting *Rinaldo* know the reason, and without taking notice that he knew any thing of his Amour; he came to him one day, and told him all the

Masters he had for the improving him in Noble Sciences were very dull, or very remiss, and that he resolved he should go for a Year or two, to the Academy at *Paris*; to this the Son made a thousand Evasions, but the Father was possitive, and not to be perswaded by all his reasons, and finding he should absolutely displease him, if he refused to go, and not daring to tell him the dear cause of his desire to remain at *Orleance*, he therefore with a breaking heart consents, to go; nay resolves it, though it should be his death; but alas! he considers that this parting, will not only prove the greatest Torment upon Earth to him, but that *Atlante* will share in his misfortune, also; this thought gives him a double Torment, and yet finds no way to evade it.

The Night that finisht this fatal day, he goes again to his wonted Station, the Window; where he had not sight very long, but he saw *Atlante* enter the Balcony, he was not able a great while to speak to her, or to utter one word, the Night was light enough to see him at the wonted place, and she admires at his silence, and demands the reason in such obliging Terms, as adds to his grief; and he with a deep sigh reply'd, urge me not my fair *Atlante* to speak, least by obeying you, I give you more cause of grief, then my silence is capable of doing, and then sighing again, he held his peace and gave her leave to ask the cause of these last words, but when he made no reply, but by sighing, she imagin'd it much worse then indeed it was, and with a trembling and fainting voice she cry'd; Oh! *Rinaldo*, give me leave to Divine that cruel news, you are so unwilling to tell me; 'tis so, added she, you are destin'd to some more Fortunate Maid than *Atlante*, at this Tears stopt her Speech, and she could utter no more, no my dearest charmer, reply'd *Rinaldo*, (Elavating his voice) if that were all, you should see with what fortitude I would dye, rather than obey any such commands; I am vow'd yours to the last moment of my Life, and will be yours in spight of all the opposition in the World, that cruelty I could evade, but cannot this that threatens me; Ah! cry'd *Atlante*, let Fate do her worst, so she till continue *Rinaldo* mine, and keep that Faith he has sworn to me intire; what can she do besides that, can afflict me? she can seperate me, cry'd he, for some time from *Atlante*. Oh! reply'd she, all misfortunes fall so below that, which I first imagin'd, that methinks, I do not resent this, as I shou'd otherwise have done; but I know when I have a little more consider'd it, I shall even dye with the grief of it, absence being so great an Enemy to Love, and makes us soon forget the Object belov'd, this though I never Experienced, I have heard and fear it may be my fate, he then convinc'd her fear with a thousand new vows, and a thousand imprecations of constancy; she then asked him, if their Loves were discover'd, that he was with such hast to depart, he told her nothing of that was the cause, and he cou'd almost wish it were discover'd since he could resolutely then refuse to go, but it was only to cultivate his Mind, more effectually than he cou'd do here, 'twas the care of his Father to accomplish him the more, and therefore he cou'd not contradict it, but, said he, I am not sent where Seas shall part us, nor vast distances of Earth, but to *Paris* , from whence he might come in two days to see her again, and that he wou'd expect from that Balcony, that had given him so many happy moments, many more, when he should come to see her, he besought her to send him away, with all the satisfaction she cou'd, which she could no otherwise do, than by giving him new assurances, that she wou'd never give away that right he had in her, to any other Lover, she vows this with innumerable Tears; and is almost angry with him for questioning her Faith; he tells her then he has but one Night more to stay, and his grief will be unspeakable, if he shou'd not be able to take a better leave of her than at a Window, and that if she wou'd give him leave, he wou'd by a Rope or two, ty'd together, so as it may serve for steps, ascend her Balcony; he not having time to provide a Ladder of Ropes: she tells him, she has so great a confidence in his verture and Love, that she will refuse him nothing, though it will be a very bold venture for a Maid, to trust her self with a passionate young Man, in silence of Night; and though she did not exert a vow from him to secure her, she expected he wou'd have a care of her Honour, he swore to her, his Love was too Religious for so base an attempt, there needed not many vows to confirm her Faith, and it was agreed on between 'em, that he should come the next Night into her Chamber.

It happen'd, that Night, as it often did, that Count *Vernole*, lay with *Monsieur De Pays*, which was in a Ground-room just under that of *Atlantes*; and as soon as she knew all were in Bed, she gave the word to *Rinaldo*, who was attending with the impatience of a passionate Lover below under the Window, and who no sooner heard the Balcony open, but he ascended with some difficulty, and enter'd the Chamber, where he found *Atlante* tremble with joy and fear: he throws himself at her Feet, as unable to speak as she, who nothing but blusht and bent down her Eyes, hardly daring to glance 'em towards the dear Object of her desires, the Lord of all her vows, she was ashamed to see a Man in her Chamber, where yet none had ever been alone, and by Night too; he saw her fear, and felt her trembling, and after a thousand sighs of Love had made way for Speech, he besought her to fear nothing from him, for his Flame was too sacred, and his passion too Holy to offer any thing, but what Honour with Love might afford him; at last he brought her to some courage, and the Roses of her fair Cheeks, assum'd their wonted Colour, not blushing too Red, nor Languishing too Pale: but when the conversation began between them, it was the softest in the World, they said all, that parting Lovers cou'd say, all that wit and tenderness cou'd express, they exchang'd their vows a new, and to confirm his, he ty'd a Bracelet of *Diamonds* about her Arm, and she return'd him one of her Hair, which he had long beg'd, and she had on purpose made, which clasped together with *Diamonds*, this she put about his Arm, and he swore to carry it to his Grave; the Night was very far spent in tender Vows, soft sighs and Tears on both sides, and it was high time to part, but as if death had been to have arriv'd to 'em in that Minute, they both linger'd away the time, like Lovers, who had forgot themselves, and day was near approaching, when he bid farwel, which he repeated very often, for still he was interrupted by some commanding softness from *Atlante*, and then lost all his Power of going, till she more couragious and careful of his interest, and her own Fame forc'd him from her, and it was happy she did so, for he was no sooner got over the Balcony, and she had flung him down his Rope, and shut the Door, but *Vernole* whom Love and Contrivance kept waking, fancy'd several times he heard a noise in *Atlantes* Chamber, and whether in passing over the Balcony, *Rinaldo* made any noise or not? or whether 'twere still his jealous fancy, he came up in his Night Gown, with a Pistol in his hand, *Atlante* was not so much lost in grief, though she were all in tears, but she heard a Man come up, and imagin'd it had been her Father, she not knowing of Count *Vernoles* lying in the House that Night, if she had, she possibly had taken more care to have ben silent, but whoever it was, she cou'd not get to Bed soon enough, and therefore turn'd her self to her dressing Table, where the Candle stood, and where lay a Book open of the story of *Ariadne* and *Thesias*, the *Count* turning the Latch, entered halting into her Chamber, in his Night Gown clapt close about him, which betray'd an ill favour'd shape, his Night-cap on, without a Periwig, which discovered all his lean wither'd Jaws, his Face pale, and his Eyes staring, and making altogether so dreadful a Figure, that *Atlante* who no more dreamt of him, then of a Devil, had possibly rather have seen the last, she gave a great screek, which frighten'd *Vernole*, so both stood for a while staring on each other, till both were recollected, he told her the care of her Honour, had brought him thither, and then rolling his small Eyes round the Chamber, to see if he cou'd discover any Body, he proceeded and cry'd *Madam*, if I had no other motive than your being up at this time of Night, or rather of Day, I cou'd easily guess how you have been entertain'd, what insolence is this, said she, all in a rage, when to cover your boldness, of approaching my Chamber at this hour, you wou'd question how I have been entertained, either explain your self, or quit my Chamber, for I do not use to see such terrible Objects here; possibly those you do see, said the *Count*, are indeed more agreeable, but I am afraid have not that regard to your Honour, as I have, and at that word, he stept to the Balcony, open'd it, and look out, but seeing no Body, he shut it too again, this inrag'd *Atlante* beyond all patience, and snatching the Pistol out of his hand, she told him, he deserved to have it aim'd at his head, for having the impudence to question her Honour, or her conduct, and commanded him to avoid her Chamber as he lov'd his Life; which she believ'd he was fonder of than of her Honour, she speaking this in a Tone wholly Transported with rage, and at the same time holding the Pistol towards him, made him tremble with fear, and he now found whether she were guilty or not, it was his turn to beg Pardon; for you must know however it came to pass, that his Jealousy made him come up in that fierce Posture, at other times *Vernole* was the most tame and passive Man in the World, and one who was afraid of his own shadow in the Night, he had a natural aversion for danger, and thought it below a Man of Wit or common Sence, to be guilty of that bruital thing called courage or fighting, his *Philosophy* told him, 'twas safe sleeping in a whole skin, and possibly he apprehended as much danger from this *Virago*, as ever he did from his own Sex, he therefore fell on his Knees, and besought her to hold her fair hand, and not to suffer that, which was the greatest mark of his respect to be the cause of her hate or indignation, the pittyful Faces he made, and the signs of mortal fear in him, had almost made her Laugh, at least it allay'd her anger, and she bid him rise and play the Fool hereafter somewhere else, and not in her presence, yet for once she would deign to give him this satisfaction, that she was got into a Book, which had many moving Stories very well writ, and that she found her self so well entertain'd, she had forgot how the Night past; he most humbly thankt her for this satisfaction and retir'd, perhaps not so well satisfy'd as he pretended.

After this he appear'd more submissive and respectful towards *Atlante*, and she carryed her self more reserved and haughty towards him, which was one reason he would not yet discover his Passion.

Thus the time ran on at *Orleance*, while *Rinaldo* found himself daily Languishing at *Paris*: he was indeed in the best Academy in the City amongst a number of brave and noble Youths. Where all things that could accomplish them, was to be learnt by those that had any Genius: but *Rinaldo* had other thoughts and other business, his time was wholly past in the most Solitary parts of the Garden, by the Melancholly Fountains, and in the most Gloomy Shades, where he could with most Liberty breath out his Passion and his Griefs, he was past the Tuterage of a Boy, and his Masters could not upbraid him, but found he had some secret cause of Grief which made him not mind these Exercises which were the delight of the rest; so that nothing being able to divert his Melancholly, which daily increas'd upon him, he fear'd it would bring him into a Fever, if he did not give himself the satisfaction of seeing *Atlante*, he had no sooner thought of this, but he was impatient to put it into Execution, he resolves to go (having very good Horses) without acquainting any of his Servants with it; he got a very handsom and light Ladder of Ropes made which he carryed under his Coat, and away he Rid for *Orleance*, stay'd at a little Village till the darkness of the Night might favour his Design, and then walking about *Atlante's* Lodgings, till he saw a light in her Chamber, and then making that noice on his Sword , 77, sig. E3] as was agreed between them, he was heard by his Adorable *Atlante*, and suffer'd to mount her Chamber: where he would stay till almost break of Day and then return to the Village, and take Horse and away for *Paris* again, this once in a Month was his Exercise without which he could not live, so that his whole Year was past in Riding between *Orleance* and *Paris*, between Excess of Grief, and Excess of Joy by turns.

'Twas now that *Atlante*, arriv'd to her Fifteenth Year, shon out with a lustre of Beauty greater than ever, and in this Year of the absence of *Rinaldo*, had carry'd her self with that severity of Life, without the youthful desire of going abroad, or desiring any Diversion, but what she found in her own retir'd thoughts, that *Vernole* wholly unable, longer to conceal his Passion, resolv'd to make a publication of it, first to the Father and then to the lovely Daughter, of whom he had some hope, because she had carried her self very well towards him for this year past, which she would never have done, if she had imagin'd he would ever have been her Lover, she had seen no signs of any such misfortune towards her in these many Years, he had convers'd with her and she had no cause to fear him: when one day her Father taking her into the Garden, told her what Honour and Happiness was in store for her, and that now the Glory of his fallen

Family would rise again, since she had a Lover of an Illustrious Blood, ally'd to *Monarchs*, and one whose Fortune was newly increas'd to a very considerable degree, answerable to his Birth, she chang'd Colour at this Discourse, imagining , 79, sig. E4] but too well, who this Illustrious Lover was, when *De Pays* proceeded and told her, indeed his Person was not the most agreeable that ever was seen, but he Marryed her to Glory and Fortune, not the Man; and a Woman, says he, ought to look no farther.

She needed not any more to inform her who this intended Husband was, and therefore bursting forth into Tears, she throws her self at his Feet, imploring him not to use the Authority of a Father, to force her to a thing so contrary to her inclinations, assuring him she could not consent to any such thing, and that she would rather dye than yield, she urg'd many Arguments, for this her Disobedience; But none would pass for current with the Old Gentleman, whose Pride had flatter'd him with hope of so considerable a Son-in-Law, he was very much surprised at *Atlantes* refusing what he believ'd she would receive with Joy, and finding that no Arguments on his side could draw her to an obedient consent, he grew to such a rage, as very rarely possest him, vowing if she did not conform her Will to his, he would Abandon her to all the Cruelty of Contempt and Poverty, so that at last she was forc'd to return him this Answer, that she would strive all she could with her Heart, but she verily believ'd she should never bring it to consent to a Marriage with *Monsieur* the *Count*: the Father continu'd threatning her, and gave her some days to consider of it; so leaving her in Tears, he return'd to his Chamber, to consider what answer he should give Count *Vernole*, whom he knew would be impatient to learn what Success he had: and , 81, sig. E5] what himself was to Hope, *De Pays* after some consideration resolv'd to tell him, she receiv'd the offer, very well; but that he must expect a little Maiden Nicety in the case, and accordingly did tell him so, and he was not at all doubtful of his good Fortune.

But *Atlante*, who resolv'd to dye a thousand Deaths rather then break her solemn Vows to *Rinaldo*, or to Marry the *Count* , cast about how she should avoid it, with the least hazard of her Fathers Rage, she found *Rinaldo* the better and more advantagious Match of the two, could they but get his Fathers Consent, he was Beautiful and Young, his Title was equal to that of *Vernole*, when his Father should dye, and his Estate exceeded his, yet she dares not make a discovery for fear she should injure her Lover, who at this time, tho she knew it not, lay sick of a Fever, while she was wondering that he came not as he us'd to do: however she resolves to send him a Letter, and acquaint him with the misfortune, which she did in these Terms.

Atlante to Rinaldo.

My Fathers Authority would force me to violate my sacred Vows to you; and give them to the Count Vernole, whom I mortally hate, yet could wish him the greatest Monarch in the World, that I might show you I could even then despise him for your sake: my Father is already too much inrag'd by my denial to hear Reason from me, if I should confess to him, my Vows to you: so that I see nothing but a prospect of Death before me, for assure your self, my Rinaldo, I will dye rather then consent to Marry any other: therefore come my Rinaldo, and come quickly, to see my Funerals, instead of those Nuptials they vainly expect from,

Your Faithful Atlante.

This Letter *Rinaldo* receiv'd, and there needed no more to make him fly to *Orleance*; this rais'd him soon from his Bed of Sickness, and getting immediately to hers, he arriv'd at his Father's House, who did not so much admire to see him, because he heard he was sick of a Fever and gave him leave to return if he pleas'd, he went directly to his Fathers House, because he knew somewhat of the business, he was resolv'd to make his passion known as soon as he had seen *Atlante*, from whom he was to take all his measures, he therefore fail'd not, when all were in Bed to rise and go from his Chamber, into the Street; where finding a light in *Atlante's* Chamber, for she every Night expected him, he made the usual sign, and she went into the Balcony, and he having no conveniency of mounting up into it, they discourst, and said all they had to say, from thence, she tells him of the *Counts* passions, of her Fathers Resolution and her own, which was rather to dye his than live any bodies else, and at last as their last refuge, they resolve to discover the whole Matter, she to her Father, and he to his, to see what Accommodation they could make, if not to dye together: They parted at this resolve, for she would not permit him longer to stay in the Street after such a sickness; so he went home to Bed but not to sleep.

The next day at Dinner *Monsigniore Bellyuard* believing his Son absolutely cur'd by absence of his passion, and speaking of all the News of the Town, among the rest, told him he was come in good time to Dance at the Wedding of *Count Vernole* with *Atlante*, the

Match being agreed on: No Sir, reply'd *Rinaldo*, I shall never Dance at the Marriage of Count *Vernole* with *Atlante*, and you will see in *Monsieur De Pays* House a Funeral sooner than a Wedding, and thereupon he told his Father all his passion, for that lovely Maid: and assur'd him if he would not see him laid in his Grave, he must consent to this Match: *Bellyuard* rose in a fury, and told him he had rather see him in the Grave then in the Arms of *Atlante*, not continued he, so much for any dislike I have to the Young Lady, or the smallness of her Fortune, but because I have so long warn'd you from such a passion, and have with such care endeavour'd by your absence to prevent it, he traverst the Room very fast, still protesting against this Aliance, and was deaf to all *Rinaldo* could say, on the other side, the day being come wherein *Atlante* was to give her final Answer to her Father, concerning her Marriage with Count *Vernole*, she assum'd all the Courage and Resolution she could to withstand the Storm, that threaten'd a Denial; and her Father came to her, and demanding her Answer; she told him, she could not be the Wife of *Vernole*, since she was Wife to *Rinaldo* , only Son to *Bellyuard*: if her Father storm'd before, he grew like a Man distracted at this Confession, and *Vernole* hearing them lowd, ran to the Chamber to learn the Cause, where just as he entered, he found *De Pays* Sword drawn and ready to kill his Daughter, who lay all in Tears at his Feet, he withheld his hand, and asking the cause of this Rage, he was told all that *Atlante* had confest, which put *Vernole* quite beside all his Gravity, and made him discover the infirmity of Anger, which he us'd to say ought to be dissembl'd by all Wise Men, so that *De Pays* forgot his own to appease his, but 'twas in vain, for he went out of the House vowing Revenge on *Rinaldo*, and to that end being not very well assur'd of his own Courage, as I said before, and being of the Opinion that no Man ought to expose his Life to him, who has injur'd him; he hir'd *Swis* and *Spanish* Souldiers to attend him in the nature of Foot-men, and watcht several Nights about *Bellyuards* Door, and that of *De Pays*, believing he should sometime or other see him under the Window of *Atlante*, or perhaps mounting into it, for now he no longer doubted, but this happy Lover was he, whom he fancy'd he heard go from the Balcony that Night, he came up with his Pistol, and being more a *Spaniard* than a *French* Man in his Nature, he resolv'd to take him any way Ungarded or Unarmed if he came in his way.

Atlante who heard his threatnings, when he went from her in a rage, fear'd his Cowardise might put him on some base Action, to deprive *Rinaldo* of his Life, and therefore thought it not safe to suffer him to come to her by Night, as he had before done; but sent him word in a Note that he should forbear her Window, for *Vernole* had sworn his Death; this Note came unseen by his Father to his Hands; but this could not hinder him from coming to her Window, which he did as soon as it was dark, he came thither, only attended with his Vallet and two Foot-men, for now he cared not who knew the Secret; he had no sooner made the sign, but he found himself incompast with *Vernoles* Bravoes; and himself standing at a distance, cry'd out, that is he: with that they all drew on both sides, and *Rinaldo* receiv'd a Wound in his Arm, *Atlante* heard this, and ran crying out that *Rinaldo* prest by numbers would be kill'd. *De Pays* who was reading in his Closet, took his Sword, and ran out, and contrary to all expectation, seeing *Rinaldo* Fighting with his back to the Door, pull'd him into the House, and fought himself with the Bravoes. Who being very much wounded by *Rinaldo*, gave ground and sheer'd off: and *De Pays* putting up Old *Billo* into the Scabbard went into his House, where he found *Rinaldo* almost Fainting with loss of Blood, and *Atlante* with her Maids binding up his Wound, to whom *De Pays* said, this Charity *Atlante* very well becomes you, and is what I can allow you; and I could wish you had no other Motive for this Action: *Rinaldo* by degrees recovered of his Fainting, and as well as his weakness would permit him, he got up and made a low Reverence to *De Pays*, telling him, he had now a double Obligation to pay him all the respect in the World, first for his being the Father of *Atlante*, and secondly, for being the Preserver of his Life, two tyes that should eternally oblige him to Love and Honour him, as his own Parent; *De Pays* reply'd, he had done nothing but what common Humanity compelled him too: but if he would make good that respect he profest towards him, it must be in quitting all hopes of *Atlante*, whom he had destin'd to another, or to an eternal inclosure in a Monastery, he had another Daughter, whom if he would think worthy of his regard, he should take his Aliance as a very great Honour, but his Word and Reputation, nay his Vows, were past to give *Atlante* to *Count Vernole*; *Rinaldo*, who before he spoke, took measure from *Atlantes* Eyes, which told him, her Heart was his; return'd this Answer to *De Pays*: that he was infinitely glad to find by the generosity of his Offer, that he had no Aversion to his being his Son-in-Law, and that next to *Atlante*, the greatest Happiness he could wish would be, his receiving *Charlot* from his hands, but that he could not think of quitting *Atlante*, how necessary soever it would be for her Glory and his —(the further) Repose: *De Pays* would not let him at this time, argue the Matter farther seeing he was Ill, and had need of looking after, he therefore begg'd he would for his Healths sake retire to his own House, whither he himself Conducted him; and left him to the care of his Men, who were escap'd the Fray; and return'd to his own Chamber, he found *Atlante* retir'd, and so he went to Bed full of Thoughts, this Night had increas'd his Esteem for *Rinaldo*, and lessen'd it for *Count Vernole*, but his Word and Honour being past, he could not break it, neither with safety nor honour; for he knew the haughty resenting Nature of the *Count*, and he fear'd some danger might arrive to the brave *Rinaldo*, which troubled him very much, at last he resolv'd, that neither might take any thing ill at his Hands, to loose *Atlante*, and send her to the Monastery where her Sister was, and compel her to be a Nun, this he thought would prevent mischiefs on both sides, and accordingly the next day (having in the Morning sent word to the Lady *Abbess* what he would have done, he carries *Atlante* under pretence of visiting her Sister, which they often did) to the Monastery, where she was no sooner come, but she was led into the inclosure, her Father he had rather Sacrifice her than she should be the cause of the Murther of two such Noble Men as *Vernole* and *Rinaldo*.

The noise of *Atlantes* being inclos'd was soon spread all over the busie Town, and *Rinaldo* was not the last to whom the News arriv'd, he was for a few days confin'd to his Chamber, where when alone, he rav'd like a Man distracted, but his Wounds had so incens'd his Father against *Atlante*, that he swore he would see his Son dye of them rather then suffer him to Marry *Atlante*, and was extreamly over-joy'd to find she was Condemn'd for ever to the Monastery, so that the Son thought it the wisest Course, and the most for the advantage of his Love, to say nothing to contradict his Father, but being almost assur'd *Atlante* would never consent to be shut up in a Cloyster and Abandon him, he flatter'd himself with hope, that he should steal her from thence, and Marry her in spight of all opposition: this he was impatient to put in Practice he believed, if he were not permitted to see *Atlante*, he had still a kind Advocate in *Charlot*, who was now arriv'd to her thirteenth Year, and infinitely advanc'd in Wit and Beauty. *Rinaldo* therefore often goes to the Monastery surrounding it, to see what possibility there was of accomplishing his Design, if he could get her Consent, he finds it not impossible, and goes to visit *Charlot*, who had command not to see him or speak to him; this was a Cruelty he lookt not for, and which gave him an unspeakable trouble, and without her aid it was wholly impossible to give *Atlante* any account of his Design, in this perplexity he remain'd many days, in which he Languisht almost to Death, he was distracted with thought, and continually hovering about the Nunnery-Walls, in hope at sometime or other to see or hear from the lovely Maid, who alone could make his Happiness, in these Traverses he often met *Vernole*, who had liberty to see her when he pleas'd, if it happen'd that they chanc'd to meet in the day time, though *Vernole* were attended with an Equipage of Ruffins, and *Rinaldo* but only with a couple of Footmen, he could perceive *Vernole* shun him, grow pale and almost tremble with fear sometimes, and get to the other side of the Street, and if he did not, *Rinaldo* having a mortal hate to him, would often bear up so close to him, that he would jostle him against the Wall, which *Vernole* would patiently put up and paseon, so that he could never be provok'd to fight by day light, how sollitary soever the place was where they met, but if they chanc'd to meet at night they were certain of Skirmish, in which he would have no part himself, so that *Rinaldo* was often like to be assassinated, but still came off with some slight Wound: this continued so long and made so great a noise in the Town, that the two Old Gentlemen were mightily Alarm'd by it, and *Count Bellyuard* came to *De Pays* one day to discourse with him of this Affair, and *Bellyuard* for the preservation of his Son, was almost consenting, since there was no Remedy, that he should Marry *Atlante*: *De Pays* confest the Honour he proffer'd him, and how troubled he was, that his word was already past to his Friend the *Count Vernole*, whom he said she should Marry or remain for ever a Nun, but if *Rinaldo* could displace his Love from *Atlante,* and place it on *Charlot* , he should gladly consent to the Match: *Bellyuard* who would now do any thing for the repose of his Son, tho he believ'd this exchange would not pass, yet resolv'd to propose it, since by Marrying him, he took him out of the Danger of *Vernole's* Assassinates, who wou'd never leave him till they had dispatcht him, should he marry *Atlante* .

While *Rinaldo* was contriving a thousand ways to come to speak to, or send Billets to, *Atlante,* none of which would succeed without the Aid of *Charlot,* his Father came and proposed this Agreement between *De Pais* and himself, to his Son. At first *Rinaldo* received it with chang'd Countenance, and a Breaking Heart; but swiftly turning from Thought to Thought, he conceiv'd this the only way to come at *Charlot,* and so consequently at *Atlante,* he therefore after some dissembl'd regret consents, with a sad put-on-Look: and *Charlot* has notice given her to see and entertain *Rinaldo,* as yet they had not told her the Reason, which her Father would tell her, when , 99, sig. F2] he came to visit her, he said, *Rinaldo* overjoy'd at this Contrivance, and his own Dissimulation, goes to the *Monastery,* visits

Charlot, where he ought to have said something of the Proposition, but wholly bent on other Thoughts, he solicits her to convey some Letters and Presents to *Atlante*, which she readily did, to the unspeakable Joy of the Poor Distrest: sometimes he would talk to *Charlot* of her own Affairs, asking her, if she resolv'd to become a *Nun*: to which she would sigh and say, if she must, it wou'd be extreamly against her Inclinations; and if it pleas'd her Father, she had rather begin the World with any Tollerable Match.

Things past thus for some Days, in which our Lovers were happy, and *Vernole* assur'd he should have *Atlante*. But at last *De Pais* came to visit *Charlot*, who ask'd her if she had seen *Rinaldo*, she answer'd, she had, and how does he entertain you, replyed *De Pais*? have you receiv'd him as a Husband? and has he behav'd himself like one? at this a suddain Joy seized the Heart of *Charlot*, and loath to confess what she had done for him to her Sister; she hung down her Blushing Face to study for an Answer: *De Pais* continu'd, and told her the Agreement between *Bellyaurd* and him, for the saving of Bloodshed: She who blest the Cause, whatever it was, having always a very great Friendship and Tenderness for *Rinaldo*, gave her Father a Thousand Thanks, for his Care, and assur'd him, since she was commanded by him, she would receive him as her Husband: and the next Day when *Rinaldo* came to visit her, as he us'd to do, and bringing a Letter with him, wherein he propos'd the Sight of *Atlante*, he found a Coldness in *Charlot*, as soon as he , 101, sig. F3] told her his Design; and desired her to carry the Letter, he ask'd the Reason of this Change, she tells him, she was inform'd of the Agreement between their two Fathers, and that she lookt upon her self as his Wife, and would act no more as a Confident, that she had ever a Violent Inclination of Friendship for him, which she would soon improve into something more Soft. He could not deny the Agreement nor his Promise, but it was in vain to tell Her, he did it only to get a Correspondence with *Atlante*; she is Obstinate, and he as pressing with all the Tenderness of Perswasion, he vows he can never be any but *Atlantes*, and she may see him die, but never break his Vows; she urges her Claim in Vain, so that at last she was overcome, and promis'd she would carry the Letter, which was to have her make her Escape that Night; he waits at the Grate for her Answer, and *Charlot* returns with one that pleased him very well, that was, that Night her Sister would make her escape, and that he must stand in such a Place of the *Nunery* Wall, and she would come out to him: after this she upbraids him with his false promise to her, and of her Goodness to serve him after such a Disappointment. He receives her Reproaches with a thousand Sighs, and bemoans his Misfortune in not being capable of more than Friendship for her, and vows, that next *Atlante* he Esteems her of all Womenkind: She seems to be obliged by this and assur'd him, she would hasten the Flight of *Atlante*, and taking leave, he went Home to order a Coach, and some Servants to assist him.

In the mean time Count *Vernole* came to visit *Atlante*, but she refused to be seen by him: and all he could do there that Afternoon , 104, sig. F4] was Entertaining *Charlot* at the Grate, to whom he spoke a great many fine things, both of her improv'd Beauty and Wit; and how happy *Rinaldo* would be in so fair a Bride, she receiv'd this with all the Civility that was due to his Quality, and their Discourse being at an end, he took his leave, it being towards the Evening.

Rinaldo wholly impatient came betimes to the Corner of the Dead Wall, where he was appointed to stand, having ordered his Foot-Men and Coach to come to him as soon as it was dark, while he was there walking up and down, *Vernole* came by the End of the Wall to go home, and looking about, he saw at the other end *Rinaldo* Walking, whose Back was towards him, but he knew him well. And though he fear'd and dreaded his Business there, he durst not encounter him, they being both attended but by one Footman a Piece. But *Vernole's* Jealousy and Indignation was so high, that he resolv'd to fetch his *Bravoes* to his aid and come and assault him; for he knew he waited there for some *Message* from *Atlante*.

In the mean time it grew dark, and *Rinaldo's* Coach came with another Footman; which were hardly arriv'd, when *Vernole* with his assistance came to the corner of the Wall, and screening themselves a little behind it, near to the place vvhere *Rinaldo* stood, vvho vvaited now close to a little door, out of vvhich the Gardners us'd to throw the Weeds and Dirt; *Vernole* could perceive anon the door to open, and a Woman come out of it, calling *Rinaldo* by his Name, vvho stept up to her, and caught her in his Arms, vvith signs of infinite Joy; *Vernole* being now all rage, cry'd to his *Assassinate*, fall on and kill the Ravisher, and immediately they all fell on; *Rinaldo*, who had only his two Footmen on his side, he was forced to let go the Lady, who would have run into the Garden again, but the door fell too and lockt; so that while *Rinaldo* was fighting, and beaten back by the *Bravoes*, one of which he laid dead at his *Feet*; *Vernole* came up to the frighted Lady, and taking her by the hand, cry'd, come my fair *Fugitive*, you must along with me; she wholly scar'd out of her

Senses, was willing to go any where out of the Terror, she heard so near her, and without reply, gave her self into his hand, who carryed her directly to her Fathers house, where she was no sooner come, but he told her *Father* all that had past, and how she was running away vvith *Rinaldo*, but that his good Fortune brought him just in the Lucky Minute, her Father turning to Reproach her found by the Light of a Candle, that this was *Charlot* and not *Atlante*; whom *Vernole* had brought Home, at which *Vernole* was Extreamly astonisht. Her Father demanded of her, why she was running away with a Man, who was designed her by consent, yes, said *Charlot*, you had his Consent Sir, and that of his Father, but I was far from getting it, I found he resolv'd to die rather then quit *Atlante*, and promising him my Assistance in his *Amour*, since he could never be mine, he got me to carry a Letter to *Atlante*, which was to desire her to fly away with him, instead of carrying her this Letter, I told her he was design'd for me, and had cancell'd all his Vows to her, she swoonded at this News, and being recover'd a little, I left her in the Hands of the *Nuns* to perswade her to live: which she resolves not to do without *Rinaldo* , tho' they press'd me, yet I resolv'd to persue my Design, which was to tell *Rinaldo*, she would obey his kind Summons, he waited for her, but I put my self into his Hands in lieu of *Atlante*, and had not the Count received me, we had been marry'd by this time, by some false Light that could not have discover'd me: But I am satisfied if I had, he would never have liv'd with me longer than the Cheat had been undiscovered, for I find them both resolv'd to die rather then change; and for my Part, Sir, I was not so much in Love with *Rinaldo* , as I was out of Love with a *Nunnery*; and took any Opportunity to quit a Life Absolutely contrary to my Humours. She spoke this with a Gayety so brisk, and an Air so agreeable, that *Vernole* found it toucht his Heart; and the rather because he found *Atlante* would never be his, or if she were, he should be still in Danger from the Resentment of *Rinaldo*; he therefore bowing to *Charlot*, and taking her by the Hand cry'd, *Madam*; since Fortune has dispos'd you thus Luckily for me, in my Possession, I humbly implore you would Consent, she should make me intirely Happy, and give me the Price for which I fought, and have conquered by my Sword; my *Lord* , reply'd *Charlot*, with a Modest Air: I am Superstitious enough to believe, that since Fortune, so contray to all our Designs, has given me into your Hands, that she from the Beginning Destined me to the Honour, which with my Fathers Consent, I shall receive as becomes me: *De Pais* Transported with Joy, to find all things would be so well brought about, it being all one to him whether *Charlot* or *Atlante* gave him Count *Vernole* for his

Son-in-Law readily consented, and immediatly a *Priest* was sent for, and they were that Night Marry'd; and it being now not above Seven a Clock, many of their Friends were invited, the Music sent for, and as good a Supper as so short a time, wou'd provide was made ready.

All this was perform'd in as short a time, as *Rinaldo* was fighting, and having kill'd one, and wounded the rest, they all fled before his Conquering Sword, which was never drawn with so good a will; when he came where his Coach stood, just against the Back-Garden Door, he lookt for his Mistriss, but the Coach-man told him, he was no sooner ingag'd, but a Man came, and with a thousand reproaches on her Levity bore her off: this made our young Lover rave, and he is satisfy'd she is in the hands of his Rival, and that he had been fighting, and Shedding his Blood, only to secure her flight with him; he lost all patience, and 'twas with much ado his Servants perswaded him to return, telling him in their Opinion, she was more likely to get out of the hands of his Rival and come to him, than when she was in the Monastery.

He suffers himself to go into his Coach, and be carry'd home, but he was no sooner alighted, but he heard Music, and a noise of Feastivals at *De Pay's* House, he saw Coaches surround his door, and Pages and Foot-men with Flamboys: this sight and noise of joy made him ready to sink down at the Door, and sending his Foot-man to learn the cause of this Triumph, the Pages that waited there, told him that Count *Vernole* was this Night Marry'd to *Monsieur De Pay's* Daughter. He needed no more to deprive him of all sense, and stagering against his Coach, he was caught by his Foot-men, and carry'd into his House; and to his Chamber, where they put him to Bed all senseless as he was, and had much ado to recover him to Life; he asked for his Father with a faint voice, for he desired to see him before he dy'd, it was told him he was gone to Count *Vernoles* Wedding, where there was a perfect peace agreed on between them, and all animosities laid aside; at this news *Rinaldo* fainted again, and his Servants called his Father home, and told him in what condition they had brought home their Master, recounting to him all that was past: he hasted to *Rinaldo*, whom he found just recover'd of his Swoonding, who putting his hand out to his Father, all cold and trembling, cry'd well Sir, now you are satisfy'd, since you have seen *Atlante* Marry'd to Count *Vernole*, I hope now you will give your unfortunate Son leave to dye, as you wisht he should rather then give him to the Arms of *Atlante*: here his Speech fail'd, and he fell again in a fit of swonding, his Father ready to dye with fear of his

Sons death, kneel'd down by his Bed side, and after having recover'd him a little, he said to him, my dear Son, I have indeed been at the Wedding of Count *Vernole*, but 'tis not *Atlante* to whom he is Marry'd, but *Charlot*, who was the Person, you were bearing from the Monastery instead of *Atlante*, who is still reserv'd for you, and who is dying till she hear you are reserv'd for her, therefore as you regard her Life, make much of your own, and make your self fit to receive her, for her Father and I have agreed the Marriage already; and without giving him leave to thank him, he call'd to one of his Gentlemen, and sent him to the Monastery, with this news to *Atlante*, *Rinaldo* bow'd himself as low as he could in his Bed, and kist the hand of his Father with tears of joy, but his weakness continu'd all next day, and they were fain to bring *Atlante* to him, to confirm his happiness.

It must only be guest by Lovers, the perfect joy these two received in the sight of each other, *Bellyuard* received her as his Daughter, and the next day made her so with very great solemnity, at which were *Vernole* and *Charlot*; between *Rinaldo* and him was concluded a perfect Peace, and all thought themselves happy in this double Union.

FINIS.